Mel Bay Presents

Jazz Album

for

Piano

12 Solos in the Style of Jazz Greats

by Misha V. Stefanuk

CD Contents

1	Afternoon Rag [5:26]	7	Sunset at the Lake [4:53]
2	Five Doughnuts Rag [2:47]	9	Brilliant Rythm [3:50]
3	Circus Rag [2:59]	9	Boogie Woogie Cat [2:36]
4	Downtown [2:35]	10	The Dancing Time [3:08]
5	Boogie Hit [3:16]	11	I Don't Think You Should [3:35]
6	Flamingo [2:58]	12	Until the Next Time I See You [2:17]

I0806898

1 2 3 4 5 6 7 8 9 0

Table of Contents

Tr. 1

Afternoon Rag

after Scott Joplin 1868-1917

Misha V. Stefanuk

Scott Joplin was born on November 24, 1868 in Texas. His first instrument was banjo, and by the age of twenty-two, he was a regular saloon pianist in St. Louis. In 1894 Joplin moved to Missouri and formed the Texas Medley Quartette, a group of eight musicians playing ragtime. One of the places Scott Joplin played was called Maple Leaf Club, and that inspired one of the best-known compositions he wrote. Another very popular piece he wrote was called "The Great Crush Collision," and it was inspired by the locomotive crash in Waco in 1896. In 1911 he moved to New York and wrote "Treemonisha," the first opera written by an African American, which received Pulitzer prize in 1976.

Scott Joplin is one of the most famous composers of Ragtime, which is a style that combines the European and African music tradition. He wrote over 60 compositions, "The Entertainer," "Weeping Willow" and "Palm Leaf Rag" being the most famous. Scott Joplin is one of the best known American composers of all time, and his music is now performed everywhere from concert halls to little clubs.

17
21
25
29
33

35
39
43
47
51

55
59
63
67
71

75
79
83
87
1.
2.
91

95
99
103
107
111

115
118
121
124
127

Tr. 2

Five Doughnuts Rag

after Jelly Roll Morton 1890-1941

Misha V. Stefanuk

Jelly Roll Morton was born on September 20, 1890 in New Orleans. His real name was Ferdinand Joseph Lemott. As a child he started playing piano in New Orleans saloons, and by the age of fifteen he was one of the most highly regarded pianists of the Storyville district. In 1904, he left New Orleans and traveled extensively through the south working as comedian, pianist and a gambler. In 1922, after spending some time in California, he moved to Chicago and made a number of very popular piano recordings. This was followed by a contract with Victor, the most influential recording label of the time. Jelly Roll formed the band Red Hot Peppers, featuring the best New Orleans musicians like Johnny Dodds and Kid Ory. In 1928, he moved to New York were he lived through some hard times during the Great Depression. Jelly Roll believed that his declining popularity and health were caused by a voodoo spell. In 1938, Alan Lomax recorded Jelly Roll Morton in a number of interviews for the Library of Congress.

Jelly Roll Morton is considered to be the first well know jazz pianist and a composer. His use of the three-minute limitation of the 78 rpm records was extraordinary and his arrangements brilliant. Among his most know compositions are "King Porter Stomp," "The Crave," and "Wolverine Blues."

17
21
25
29
33

37
41
45
49
53

57
61
65
69
73

77
81
85
89
94

Tr. 3

Circus Rag

after Thomas Fats Waller 1904-1943

Misha V. Stefanuk

Thomas "Fats" Waller was born in New York on May 2, 1904. His first teachers were his mother, who taught him how to play church music on the organ, and the pianola, a player piano which showed him how to play ragtime. As a boy, Thomas sang in the choir of Abyssinian Baptist Church in Harlem. In 1918 he won a contest playing "Carolina Stout," which he transcribed from the pianola. The connection with the composer of the song, James P. Johnson was established after that competition. Fats took piano lessons from him, and later the two wrote music together for Johnson's show "Keep Shufflin."

The most known Fats Waller's song, "Ain't Misbehavin,'" is a part of the 1930 musical "Hot Chocolates" featuring Louis Armstrong. In 1932, Fats got his own radio show called "Fats Waller's Rhythm Club" in Cincinatti. Two years later he moved to New York and the show got much wider exposure. At a party at George Gershwin's house he met an executive from Victor, the largest recording company of the time, who decided to replace Jelly Roll Morton's Red Hot Peppers with Fats Waller's Rhythm Club, now called Fats Waller and his Rhythm. The group recorded sometimes up to ten songs per day and had many best selling albums. Fats also toured United States and Europe. The last recording of Fats Waller and his Rhythm was released in 1942.

Fats Waller continued his studies of music and playing theater and church organ throughout his life. He is considered to be one of the best selling jazz pianists of all time.

13
16
19
22
25

28
31
34
37
40

43
46
49
52
55

58
61
64
67
70

73
76
79
82
85

88
91
94
97
100

Tr. 4

Downtown

after Count Basie 1904-1984

Misha V. Stefanuk

William Basie was born in Red Bank, New Jersey on August 21, 1904. His first piano teacher was his German nanny. In 1920, he moved to Harlem where he listened to jazz pianists like Fats Waller and James P. Johnson. In 1927, he got a job playing for silent movies and later played with the Blue Devils and the Bennie Morton Band. In 1935 he returnd to Kansas City, and after winning a radio competition he started recording with his own band, the Barons of Rhythm. Many famous jazz musicians started with this band including Lester Young, Thad Jones and Jo Jones.

The band played on and off throughout the 1970's, performing with stars from Tony Bennett and Sarah Vaughan to Frank Sinatra and Bing Crosby. One of Basie's great recordings is a duo album with Oscar Peterson.

Count Basie has changed the face of ensemble playing in terms of arranging for the jazz band using riffs and the rhythm section. He also developed a very minimal piano accompaniment style called comping.

17
21
25
29
33

37
41
45
49
53

57
3
61
3
3
65
3
69
73

Tr. 5

Boogie Hit

after Pete Johnson 1904-1967

Misha V. Stefanuk

Pete Johnson was born on March 24, 1904 in Kansas City, Missouri. At the age of three, his mother put him in an orphanage where he stayed until the age of twelve. Pete started playing drums at the age of eighteen and had a few gigs as a drummer. In 1926 he started working as a pianist, learning how to play the instrument from his uncle. Sunset Club in Missouri became the place to be seen as a musician, and the famous blues song, "Roll'em Pete" was inspired by excited audiences yelling, "Roll'em Pete!"

In 1938 Pete Johnson played a concert at Carnegie Hall in a series called Spirituals to Swing along with Albert Ammons and Meade Lux Lewis. Later these three formed a group called The Boogie Woogie Trio. In 1947 he moved to Los Angeles and in 1950 to Buffalo New York. In 1958, he played the famous Newport Jazz Festival. Pete Johnson had a stroke in 1958, and he performed publicly in 1967 playing the right hand only. Peter (Pete) Johnson was a leading American boogie-woogie player.

14
17
20
23
26

29
32
35
38
41

44
47
50
53
57

60
63
66
3
69
72

Tr. 6

Flamingo

after Duke Ellington 1899-1974

Misha V. Stefanuk

Edward Kennedy Ellington was born on April 29, 1899 in Washington, D.C. He began piano lessons at a young age from his parents but was more interested in baseball. Later he was inspired by jazz, and he started playing again and formed his first group by the age of eighteen.

In 1923, Duke Ellington moved to New York and shortly after appeared nationwide on the radio in the program "From the Cotton Club." Duke Ellington's band performed with Dizzy Gillespie, Cab Calloway, Louis Armstrong and Ella Fitzgerald among many others. Among the numerous hits Ellington recorded for Columbia Records are "Satin Doll," "Take the A Train" and "The Mooche." Duke Ellington's band traveled internationally from Cairo and Moscow to London and Paris. His influence as a serious composer is also very important, he was the first composer of the large-scale orchestral jazz composition with three-movements, Black, Brown and Beige, written in 1943.

Duke Ellington was one of the greatest American composers and pianists. He wrote, arranged and recorded hundreds of tunes that became standards played all around the globe. Duke Ellington was honored by the French Legion, and received the American Presidential Medal of Honor.

19
23
27
3
31
35

39
3
3
42
45
48
51
3

Sunset at the Lake

after Erroll Garner 1921(23)-1977

Misha V. Stefanuk

Erroll Garner was born between 1921 and 1923 in Pittsburgh, Pennsylvania. According to different sources he started playing piano by ear at the age of either two or three. Like Fats Waller, he learned his first popular music pieces listening to records, 78's instead of pianola however. When Erroll was seven, he first appeared on the radio with his group called Candy Kids. By eleven he had a regular job playing piano on riverboats.

In his twenties, Erroll Garner moved to New York and started recording and touring. Garner's style is very recognizable, mainly because of the repetitive left hand part that is derived from simplified ragtime but also uses a strong accents, reminiscent of comping style and his right hand playing block chords. Among his other brilliant recordings, Erroll Garner recorded the best selling piano jazz album called "Concert by the Sea."

29
3
32
35
38
41

44
47
50
53
55

59
62
65
67
70

72
74
77
3
3
80
83

86
91

This page has been left blank
to avoid awkward page turns.

Tr. 8

Brilliant Rythm

after Art Tatum 1909-1956

Misha V. Stefanuk

Art Tatum was born on October 13, 1909 in Toledo, Ohio. He went to the Toledo School of Music, but due to his almost complete blindness, he was mostly self-taught. Tatum's first influence was the music of Fats Waller, which like Erroll Garner and Fats, he learned by listening to records. At the age of eighteen, Art was hired by a local radio station and given his own show. At the age of twenty-four, Art Tatum moved to New York and started working as an accompanist as well as recording his own original material. Art developed an extremely fast technique of playing arpeggios and scales, and he became famous for winning piano competitions with other great pianists in New York. In the 1940's, Art Tatum's trio toured extensively in the United States and Europe. 1954 brings the contract with famous producer Norman Granz, who is also responsible for a whole line of amazing jazz recordings. Some of Art Tatum's recordings feature him playing in ensembles with other jazz greats, and some of them feature Art playing solo. There are even recordings of him playing classical pieces, like Dvoräk's Humoresque, on which he also improvises.

Art Tatum is one of the most well-known and highly regarded American pianists. While listening to his records, his brilliant technique made generations of pianists gasp. However his influence on others was also limited due to the incredibly difficult technique he developed and refined. In 1938, Fats Waller announced that he is just playing piano but God is in the house tonight, referring to Art being in the audience.

13
3
3
3
16
19
22
25

28
31
34
37
40
5

43
46
49
52
55

58
61
64
67
70

73
76
79
82
85

88
91
94
97
100
5

103
106
109

Tr. 9

Boogie Woogie Cat

after Oscar Peterson b.1925

Misha V. Stefanuk

Oscar Peterson was born on August 15, 1925 in Montreal, Quebec. He started learning trumpet and piano from his father at the age of five. About two years later he switched to piano only, mostly because of health reasons. At the age of fifteen, he started taking lessons from Paul de Marky, a famous classical pianist. Oscar started appearing on the radio, eventually getting his own program "Fifteen Minute Radio Rambling." At the age of twenty-two, Oscar Peterson formed his first trio and received a recording contract with RCA. About to years later, Peterson appeared at Carnegie Hall, which starts his relationship with Norman Granz. He toured the world and made probably the most influential recordings of all jazz pianists. In 1958 he moved back to Toronto.

The influence Oscar Peterson's playing has on jazz pianists is unmistakable. For generations young jazz pianists wanted nothing more than to sound like Oscar Peterson. His influence is also enourmous as a composer. He wrote a number of large scale jazz works like "Canadiana Suite" and "Hymn to Freedom." He wrote scores for movies and hosted the TV shows Oscar Peterson Presents, CTV and Piano Party, BBC. Among honors that Oscar Peterson has received are the Canadian Film Award, seven Grammies and eleven Grammy nominations, ten Honorary Doctorates, Officer of the Order of Canada, Officer of Arts and Letters and Toronto Arts Award for Lifetime Achievement.

13
16
19
3
3
22
25

28
31
34
37
40

43
46
49
52
55

58
61
64
67
70

This page has been left blank
to avoid awkward page turns.

Tr. 10

The Dancing Time

after Dave Brubeck b.1920

Misha V. Stefanuk

Dave Brubeck was born in Concord, California on December 6, 1920. His first piano teacher was his mother, and he started playing popular tunes by ear around the age of four. When Dave was 11, the family moved to a ranch near Ione, and he decided that he wanted to be a rancher. However by age 15, he also started playing dances in neighboring cities, and at 18 he left for college. After the first year of study, Brubeck's original idea of becoming a veterinarian was replaced by playing piano, and he changed his major to music. In 1942, Brubeck was drafted and went into the army, once again to find himself playing piano. After the war Dave Brubeck went to Mills College to study under famous French classical composer Darius Millhaud. The influence of Millhaud in Brubeck's music is evident, he is one of the rare jazz composers to use polyrhythm and polytonality, which are trademarks of French contemporary music.

In 1958 Brubeck formed the Dave Brubeck Quartet that records "Take Five," "It's a Raggy Waltz" and "Blue Rondo a la Turk" and continued performing and recording for the next ten years. Also Brubeck's outcome as a composer is quite significant. Like Duke Ellington and Oscar Peterson he wrote large-scale works, but much of his music is purely classical. Dave Burbeck wrote four cantatas, a mass, two ballets and a musical among many solo and orchestral pieces. Dave Brubeck holds four honorary doctorates, BMI Jazz Pioneer Award and American Eagle Award and his musical and personal influence on contemporary jazz is unmistakable.

16
3
19
3
22
3
26
31

34
3
3
37
41
45
49

53
57
61
65
69
3

73
76
3
3
79
82
3
3
85

90
94
97
3
3
101
106

Tr. 11

I Don't Think You Should

after Thelonius Monk 1917-1982

Misha V. Stefanuk

Thelonious Sphere Monk was born on October 10, 1917 in Red Row, Rocky Mount, North Carolina. In 1923, his family moved to New York where he grew up. Around 1927, Monk started taking piano lessons and soon played for his family's church choir. In 1934, he went on tour with a religious group. After his return home, Monk went to Julliard and got a job playing for Teddy Hill. Working at Minton's he met Dizzy Gillespie, Coleman Hawkins, Kenny Clark and Charlie Parker, which led to Monk's playing with the Cootie Williams Orchestra and Dizzy Gillespie's Big Band. In 1944, Monk recorded with Coleman Hawkins and in 1947 with Art Blakey and Milt Jackson. In 1951, the recording for the Blue Note contains "Straight, No Chaser" and "'Round Midnight," probably the two best known of Monk's compositions. The same year Monk lost his right to perform in New York City due to a drug problem, which he continued for the next 6 years. In 1955, Monk's trio records a tribute to Duke Ellington, which starts his return to the mainstream jazz scene. In the following years, Monk recorded with Clark Terry, John Coltrane, Thad Jones, Gerry Mulligan and Clark Terry.

In 1962, Monk signed with Columbia and recorded a series of albums. In 1964, Monk was on the cover of Time, and he toured with Phil Woods and Clark Terry. After a 1971 tour with the "Giants of Jazz," Thelonius Monk stopped performing publicly and died on February 17, 1982. Monk's influence on contemporary music is even more important as a composer than as a pianist. He has been called the next great composer after Bartok. His charismatic persona continues to be very popular among younger jazz musicians. He fought the same demons that many musicians have to face, being extremely talented and dealing with racism, drugs and alcohol. Many of Monk's tunes from "Round Midnight" to "Well You Needn't" are played constantly in jam sessions, concerts and recordings, and have since become jazz standards.

37
41
45
3
49
53

57
61
65
69
73

77
81

Tr. 12

Until the Next Time I See You

after Bill Evans 1929-1980

Misha V. Stefanuk

William John Evans was born on August 16, 1929 in Plainfield, New Jersey. As a child Bill studied classical violin, cello, flute and piano. While attending Southeastern Louisiana University, he started playing with a number of dixieland bands and played with Red Mitchell and Charles Mingus. In 1956, he formed his trio with Scott La Faro and Paul Motian, both virtuoso instrumentalists sharing a love for classical music. 1958 brought work with Miles Davis, which resulted in "Kind of Blue" one year later. Until La Faro's tragic death, the trio recorded four albums, including the "Village Vanguard" recordings. Bill Evans continued to work with the trio through most of his life; Eddie Gomez took over the bass part from 1966 to 1967. The trio developed a very rare form of melodic, rhythmic and harmonic conversation that influenced generations of musicians. Starting with playing standards Bill Evans continued to write very complicated and intricate original compositions. Besides the trio, Bill Evans worked with a number of musicians including Jimm Hall, Cannonball Adderley, Jack DeJohnette and Tony Bennett, and also recorded a series of multi-tracked piano recordings.

Bill Evans is a very unique figure in jazz. His love for French impressionist music influenced his compositions and his playing, resulting in the development of a very personal harmonic style and a very lyrical and sophisticated piano technique. His music was always welcomed by jazz fans and non-jazz audiences alike. Bill Evans died on September 15, 1980 and one year later was elected into the Down Beat Hall of Fame.

17
21
25
29
3
33

37
41

About the Author

Mel Bay best-selling author, Misha V. Stefanuk, started playing piano at the age of five. He composed his first piece when he was nine. Mr. Stefanuk studied at the Moscow Studio of Music Improvisation Art, the Moscow Conservatory School, the Russian Academy of Music, Belmont University, Skidmore Jazz Institute, and Washington State University. He has written more then 100 works for a variety of instrumentations, as well as music for over thirty theater shows, including an original score for *Y2K Survival Guide* with Leonard Nimoy. Misha has composed a significant amount of music for network television, including programs such as *All My Children* (ABC), *One Life to Live* (ABC), *Passions* (NBC), *The Chris Isaak Show* (Showtime) and *First Monday* (CBS). Among his works are the Mel Bay best-sellers *Jazz Piano Chords* (98713) and *Jazz Piano Scales & Modes* (98715).

Mr. Stefanuk is a monthly columnist for *Creative Keyboard* and a judge at the "Annual Chopin Youth Piano Competition" in Milwaukee, Wisconsin. Mr. Stefanuk is a prize-winner of the Stereotypes and Nations Composition Competition held by Muzica Centrum Art Society in Cracow, Poland for his composition *Equinokse* for oboe, string trio and prepared piano, and winner of the Concerto Aria Composition Competition at Belmont University for his piece *The New American Symphony.* He was also named Outstanding Piano Player at the 129th Annual Lionel Hampton Jazz Festival, and has won full scholarships at Belmont University, Washington State University, and Skidmore Summer Jazz Institute.

Misha and his wife, Evan, teach over 100 students at Johnson Ferry Conservatory of Music in Atlanta, Georgia and privately. Among them are recording artists, TV personalities, winners of national and regional competitions, and teachers. Misha's students attended a number of prestigious music schools in US, and abroad. Mr. Stefanuk has released over 20 CDs varying from contemporary classical to jazz, new age and pop.

Visit Misha's web site at www.stefanuk.com

photo by Scot Lewis